READING IS FUN
WITH Dr. Seuss

CONTENTS

Hop on Pop

Marvin K. Mooney Will You Please Go Now!

Oh, The Thinks You Can Think!

I Can Read With My Eyes Shut!

The Cat in the Hat
TM & © Dr. Seuss Enterprises, L.P. 1957
All Rights Reserved

This omnibus edition first published in the UK 2001.
This edition published 2004 by HarperCollins *Children's Books*,
a division of HarperCollins*Publishers* Ltd,
77-85 Fulham Palace Road, Hammersmith, London W6 8JB

The HarperCollins children's website address is:

www.harpercollins.co.uk

13 15 17 19 20 18 16 14

ISBN : 978 0 00 719207 6

Reading is Fun with Dr. Seuss
Hop on Pop © 1963, 1991 by Dr. Seuss Enterprises, L.P.
All Rights Reserved.
Published by arrangement with Random House Inc.,
New York, USA
First published in the UK 1964
Marvin K. Mooney Will You Please Go Now! © 1972, 2000 by Dr. Seuss Enterprises, L.P.
All Rights Reserved
Published by arrangement with Random House Inc.,
New York, USA
First published in the UK 1973
Oh, The Thinks You Can Think! © 1975, 2003 by Dr. Seuss Enterprises, L.P.
All Rights Reserved
Published by arrangement with Random House Inc.,
New York, USA
First published in the UK 1976
I Can Read With My Eyes Shut! © 1978 by Dr. Seuss Enterprises, L.P.

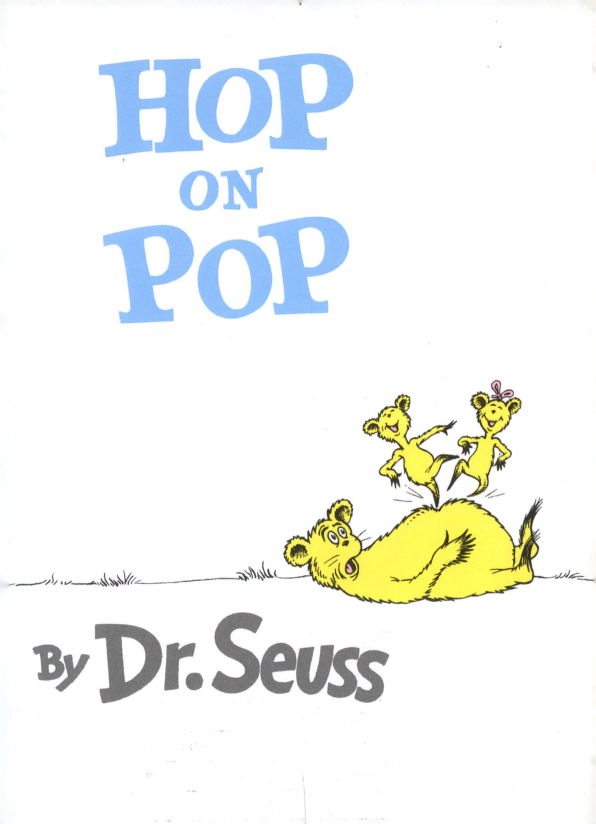

UP
PUP

Pup is up.

CUP
PUP

Pup in cup

PUP
CUP

Cup on pup

MOUSE
HOUSE

Mouse on house

HOUSE
MOUSE

House on mouse

ALL
TALL

We all are tall.

ALL
SMALL

We all are small.

ALL
BALL

We all play ball

BALL
WALL

up on a wall.

ALL
FALL

Fall off the wall

DAY
PLAY

We play all day.

NIGHT FIGHT

We fight all night.

HE
ME

He is after me.

HIM
JIM

Jim is after him.

SEE
BEE

We see a bee.

SEE
BEE
THREE

Now we
see three.

THREE
TREE

Three fish in a tree

Fish in a tree?
How can that be?

RED
RED

They call me Red.

RED
BED

I am in bed.

RED
NED
TED
and
ED
in
BED

PAT
PAT

They call him Pat.

PAT
SAT

Pat sat on hat.

PAT
CAT

Pat sat on cat.

PAT
BAT

Pat sat on bat.

NO
PAT
NO

Don't sit on that.

SAD

DAD

BAD

HAD

Dad is sad
very, very sad.
He had a bad day.
What a day Dad had!

THING
THING

What is that thing?

THING
SING

That thing can sing!

SONG
LONG

A long, long song

Good-by, Thing.
You sing too long.

WALK
WALK

We like to walk.

WALK
TALK

We like to talk.

HOP
POP

We like to hop.
We like to hop
on top of Pop.

STOP

You must not
hop on Pop.

Mr. BROWN
Mrs. BROWN

Mr. Brown upside down

Pup up

Brown down

Pup is down.
Where is Brown?

WHERE IS BROWN?
THERE IS BROWN!

Mr. Brown is out of town.

BACK
BLACK

Brown came back.

Brown came back
with Mr. Black.

SNACK
SNACK

Eat a snack.

Eat a snack
with Brown and Black.

JUMP
BUMP

He jumped.
He bumped.

FAST
PAST

He went past fast.

WENT
TENT
SENT

He went into the tent.

I sent him out of the tent.

WET
GET

Two dogs get wet.

HELP
YELP

They yelp for help.

HILL
WILL

Will went up the hill.

WILL

HILL

STILL

Will is
up the hill still.

FATHER
MOTHER

SISTER
BROTHER

That one is
my other brother.

My brothers read
a little bit.

Little
words
like

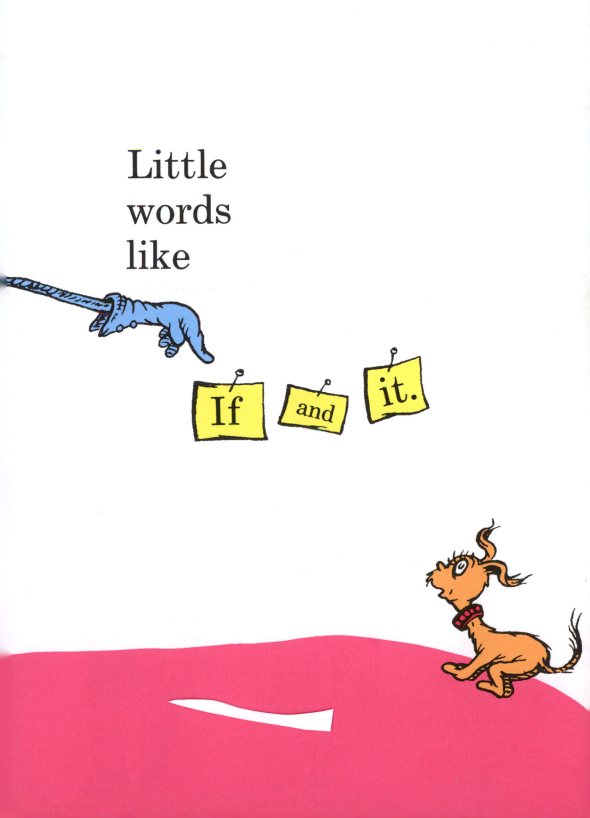

If and it.

My father
can read
big words, too

like...............

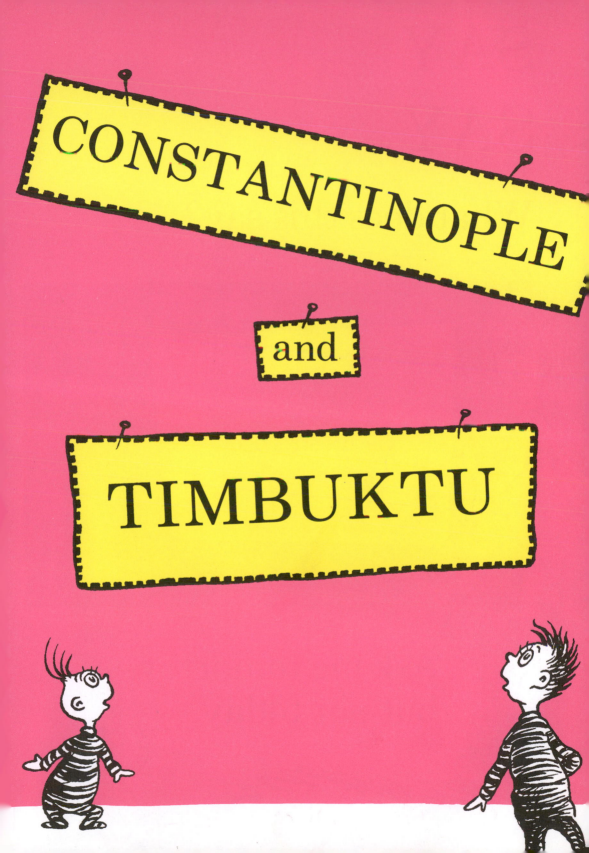

SAY
SAY

What does this say?

seehemewe
patpuppop
hethreetreebee
tophopstop

Ask me tomorrow
but not today.

Marvin K. Mooney Will you

PLEASE

GO

NOW!

By Dr. Seuss

The
time
has come.

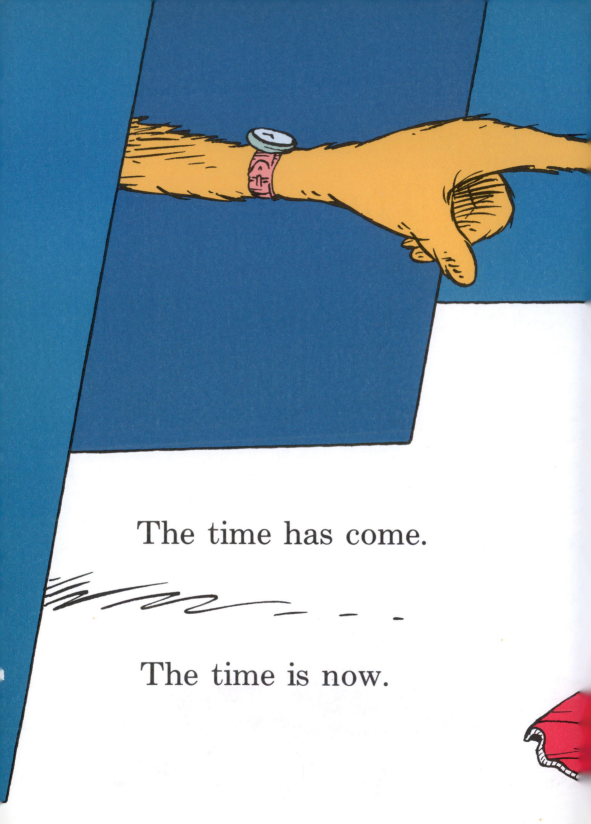

The time has come.

The time is now.

Just go.
Go.
GO!
I don't care how.

You can go by foot.

You can go
by cow.

Marvin K. Mooney,
will you
please go now!

You can go
on skates.

You can go
on skis.

You can go
in a hat.

But
please go.
Please!

I don't care.
You can go
by bike.

You can go
on a Zike-Bike
if you like.

If you like
you can go
in an old blue shoe.

Just go, go, GO!
Please do, do, DO!

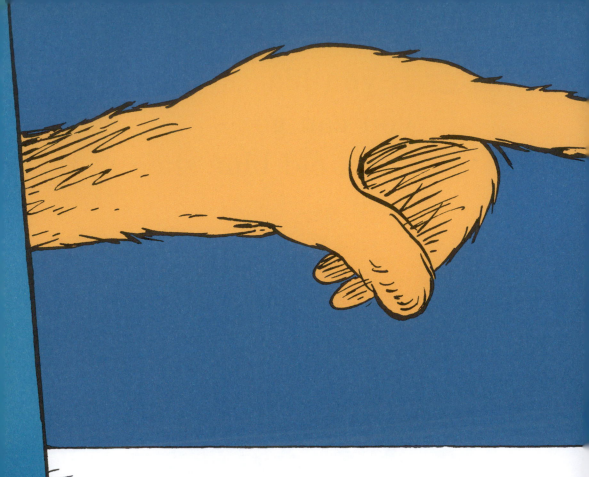

Marvin K. Mooney,
I don't care how.
Marvin K. Mooney,
will you please
GO NOW!

You can go on stilts.

You can go by fish.

You can go
in a Crunk-Car
if you wish.

If you wish
you may go
by lion's tail.

Or stamp yourself
and go by mail.

Marvin K. Mooney!
Don't you know
the time has come
to go, Go, GO!

Get on your way!
Please, Marvin K.!
You might like going
In a Zumble-Zay.

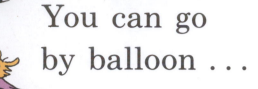

You can go
by balloon ...

... or broomstick.

OR

You can go
by camel
in a
bureau drawer.

You can go by Bumble-Boat . . .

. . . or jet.

I don't care
how you go.

Just GET!

Get yourself a Ga-Zoom.

You can go with a ....

Marvin, Marvin, Marvin!
Will you leave this room!

Marvin K. Mooney!
I don't care HOW.

Marvin K. Mooney!

Will you please

GO NOW!

I said

GO

and

GO

I meant. . . .

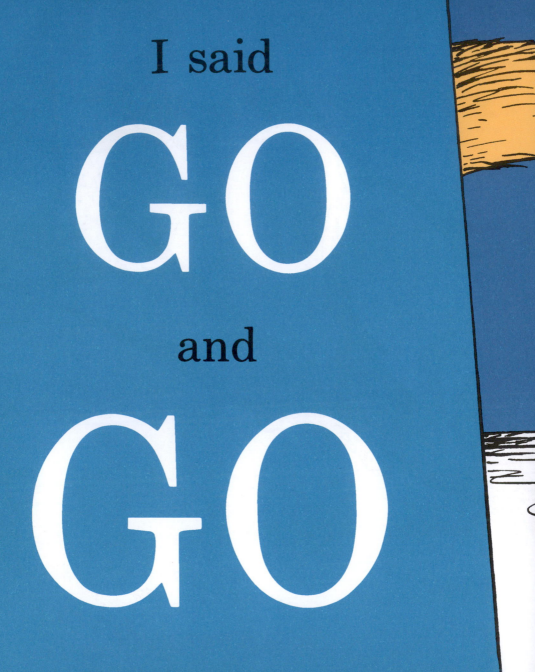

The time had come.
SO . . .
Marvin WENT.

Oh, the THINKS you Can Think!

by Dr. Seuss

You can

think up

some birds.

That's what you can do.

You can think about yellow

or think about blue . . .

You can think about red.
You can think about pink.
You can think up a horse.
Oh, the THINKS you can think!

Oh, the THINKS
you can think up
if only you try!

If you try,
you can think up
a GUFF going by.

And you don't have to stop.

You can think about SCHLOPP.

Schlopp. Schlopp. Beautiful schlopp.

Beautiful schlopp

with a cherry on top.

You can think about gloves.
You can think about SNUVS.

You can think a long time
about snuvs and their gloves.

You can think about
Kitty O'Sullivan Krauss
in her big balloon swimming pool
over her house.

Think of black water.

Think up a white sky.

Think up a boat.

Think of BLOOGS blowing by.

You can think about Night,
a night in Na-Nupp.
The birds are asleep
and the three moons are up.

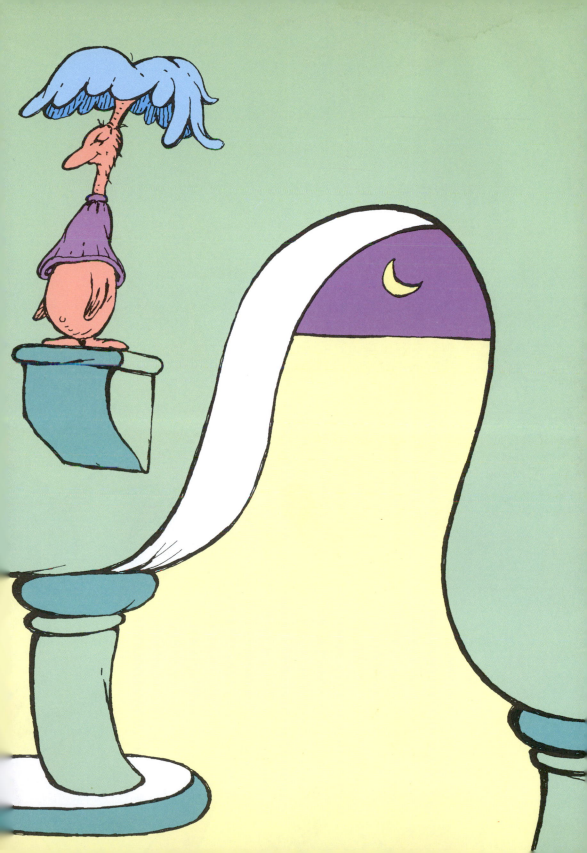

You can think about Day,
a day in Da-Dake.
The water is blue
and the birds are awake.

Think! Think and wonder.

Wonder and think.

How much water

can fifty-five elephants drink?

You can wonder . . .

How long
is the tail
of a ZONG?

There are so many THINKS
that a Thinker can think!

Would you dare
yank a tooth
of the
RINK-RINKER-FINK?

And
what would
you do
if
you met
a JIBBOO?

Oh, the THINKS
you can think!

Think of
Peter the Postman
who crosses the ice
once every day—
and on Saturdays, twice.

THINK! You can think
any THINK
that you wish . . .

Think
a race
on a horse
on a ball
with a fish!

Think of Light.
Think of Bright.
Think of
Stairs in the Night.

THINK!

Think a ship.

Think up a long trip.

Go visit the VIPPER,

the Vipper of Vipp.

And left!

Think of Left!

And think about BEFT.
Why is it that beft
always go to the left?

And why is it
so many things
go to the Right?
You can think about THAT
until Saturday night.

Think left and think right
and think low and think high.
Oh, the THINKS you can think up if only you try!

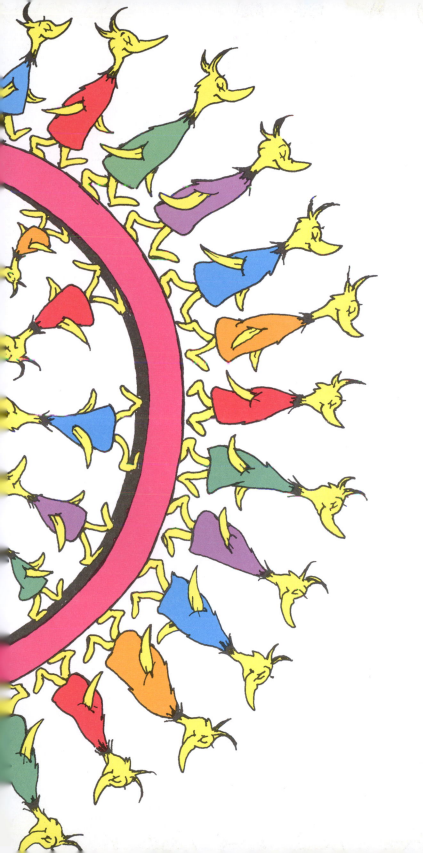

I Can Read with My Eyes Shut!

By Dr. Seuss

For

David Worthen, E.G.*

*(Eye Guy)

I can read
in **red.**

I can read
in **blue.**

I can read in
pickle colour
too.

I can read in bed.

And in **purple.**
And in **brown.**

I can read
with
my
left eye.

I
can
read
with
my right.

I can read
Mississippi
with my eyes shut tight!

Mississippi

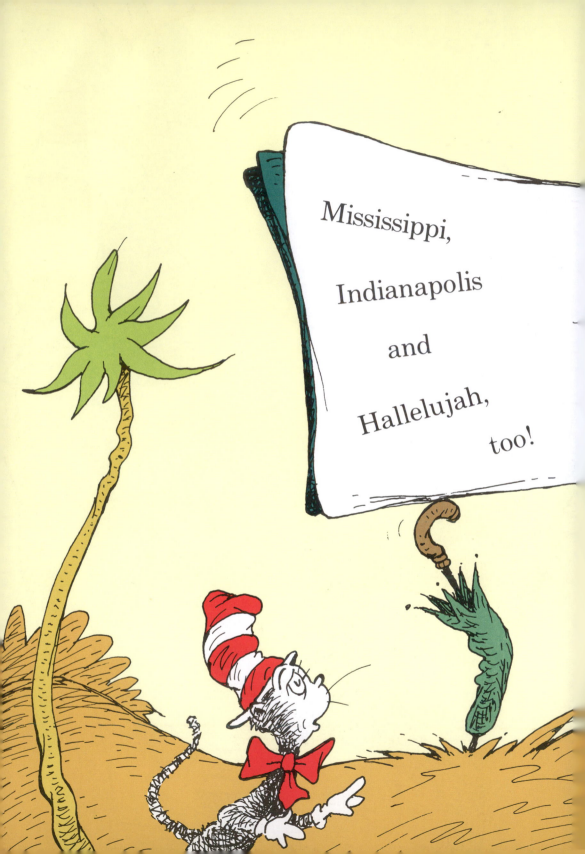

Mississippi,

Indianapolis

and

Hallelujah,

too!

I can read them
with my eyes shut!

That is

VERY HARD

to do!

But it's bad for my hat
and makes my eyebrows
get red hot.

so . . .

reading with my eyes shut
I don't do an awful lot.

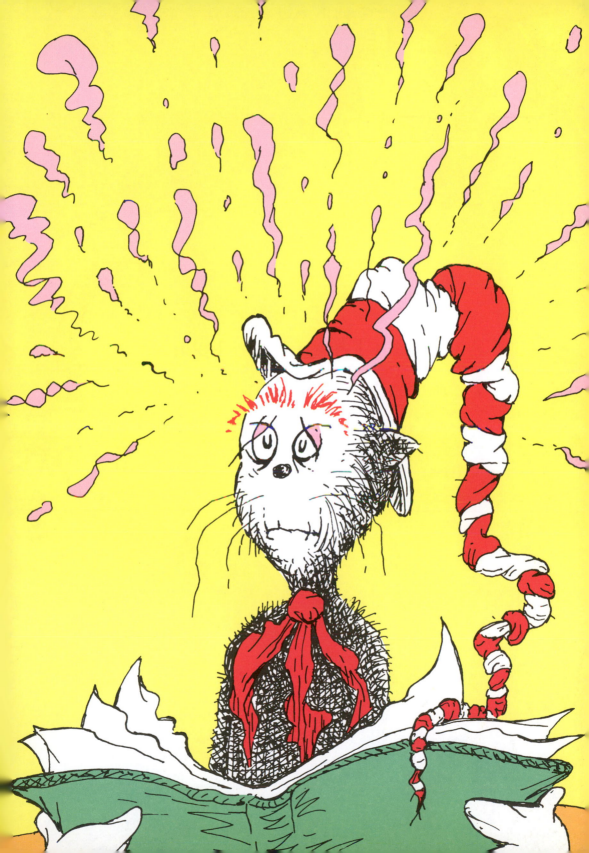

And when I keep them open
I can read with much more speed.
You have to be a speedy reader
'cause there's so, so much to read!

You can read about anchors.

And all about ants.

You can read
about ankles!

And crocodile pants!

You can read about hoses . . .

and how
to smell roses . . .

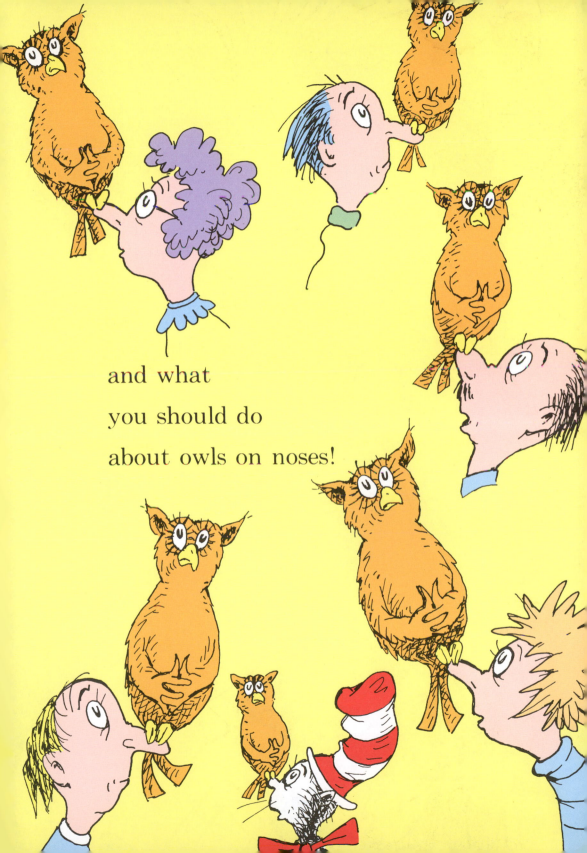

and what

you should do

about owls on noses!

Young cat! If you keep
your eyes open enough,
oh, the stuff you will learn!
The most wonderful stuff!

You'll learn about . . .

 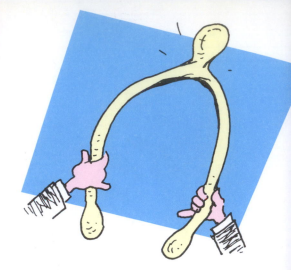

fishbones . . . and wishbones.

You'll learn about trombones, too.

You'll learn
about Jake
the Pillow Snake

and all about
Foo-Foo the Snoo.

You can learn about ice.
You can learn about mice.

Mice on ice.

And
ice
on
mice.

You can learn about
the price of ice.

Nice ice
for sale.
Ten cents a pail.

You can learn about SAD . . .

and GLAD . . .

and MAD!

OUT

IN

There are
so many things
you can learn about.
BUT . . . you'll miss
the best things
if you keep
your eyes shut.

The more that you read,

the more things you will know.

The more that you learn,

the more places you'll go.

You might learn

a way to earn

a few dollars.

Or how to make doughnuts . . .

or kangaroo collars.

You can learn to read music
and play a Hut-Zut
if you keep your eyes open.
But <u>not</u> with them shut.

If you read with your eyes shut
you're likely to find
that the place where you're going
is far, far behind.

SO . . .

that's why I tell you

to keep your eyes wide.

Keep them wide open . . .

at least on one side.